I0724751

PULPED FICTION

an anthology of microlit

edited by

Cassandra Atherton

SPINELESS WONDERS
www.shortaustralianstories.com.au

Spineless Wonders
PO Box 220
STRAWBERRY HILLS
New South Wales, Australia, 2012
shortaustralianstories.com.au

First published by Spineless Wonders 2021
Text copyright © remains with individual authors.
Cover image and design by Bettina Kaiser

Editorial assistance by Meredith Tyler. Layout by Bronwyn Mehan.

Typeset in Franklin Gothic Book
Printed and bound by Ingram Spark
ISBN 9781925052602

Pulped Fiction, an anthology of microlit/
Atherton, Cassandra (ed)

Distribution in Australia and New Zealand by New South

A catalogue record for this book is available from the National Library of Australia

'Just because you are a character doesn't mean
that you have character.'
PULP FICTION

Contents

Introduction

Iconic romance author Nora Roberts once described writing category romance fiction as trying to perform Swan Lake in a phone booth. I was reminded of this metaphor several times as I was reading *Pulped Fiction*, because it also encapsulates the challenge facing the writers here: to invoke all the intertextual layers of meaning inherent in genre within an incredibly tiny space.

Successful genre writing must balance two things: expectation and surprise. Audiences have expectations of genre – the crime novel without a crime is no crime novel at all. But they also want to be surprised, to be astonished. They know the romance will end happily, or the crime will be solved, or the princess woken from her slumber, but they do not know how the story will get there, and that journey is where the fun lies.

In *Pulped Fictions*, within these tiny phone booths, the usual expectations of genre are invoked, negotiated and hybridised in playful, surprising ways. One of the charges commonly levelled at popular genre fiction is that it is stale and unimaginative, but in this collection, we see the ways in which its rich levels of meaning can be brought to bear in fresh and exciting ways. Each version of Swan Lake within these covers is different, thrilling, new – while still being intensely familiar.

This is a wonderfully evocative volume, and by playing with genre, it encourages us to think about how the expectations we've learned from it shape the way we think and narrativise our own lives: You phone to say there's a man following far too close and you can't tell if it's thriller, romance or porn, writes Jen Webb in 'Earth Enraged by New Humans'. Genres are imbued with deep strata of meaning and feeling. In *Pulped Fictions*, readers may enjoy excavating some of them.

Jodi McAlister, 2021

joanne burns

DEATH OF A GOTH

virginia felt pretty heady when she entered the pantry after a morning amongst the butterflies in the garden at monk's house. cook had just left to attend a funeral and would be absent for two days. virginia had plans to make a batch of scones for tse's visit to talk about a new edition of 'the waste land'. 'oh no' she shrieked. she hadn't expected to find the flour full of pantry moths. pantry moths! those little vandals. waves of them coming at her.

she had forgotten how to kill them.

'lenny lenny' she called. leonard should remember how to get rid of these pests. after all he'd had plenty of bug experience in ceylon. but he couldn't hear her. he was down by the river reading a biography of ramakrishna. his ears were full of bhakti. maybe she should telephone vita over at sissi. but she might laugh at her, assure her that they would die in the oven. just little specks really.

then virginia had a lightbulb moment. that bottle of ether tom and viv had left behind on the guest room mantlepiece last visit should knock them out. there'd still be time to make the scones.

she'd serve them with peach jam.

Jen Webb

EARTH ENRAGED BY NEW HUMANS

When you begged for change, you didn't mean this: a world that is all change. New laws mean old growth, but laws keep fading from the screens, and the beaded folk appear in the forests, setting up camp.

She says, *I thought I had a pretty good handle on things, but now I can't tell what sort of story I'm in.* He draws her feet onto his lap, finds the pressure points, kneads away the fears. Later he takes her to bed where she repays him, with interest.

The underground is fighting back. A tree has stolen my password, and now I can't open emails. A tree cracked my mum's computer and has emptied her accounts. It's what the scientists warned us: the forests are angry – by day, mildmannered plants, respiring and photosynthesizing; by night, maquis, encrypting messages, breaking codes.

All the genres are breaking their codes. You phone to say there's a man following far too close and you can't tell if it's thriller, romance or porn. I tell you that the toothpaste disappeared from my grocery cart, and was nowhere to be found. *Is there meaning in this?* we ask each other. *Are we in some cli-fi tale?*

High in the mother tree a meliorist is swinging from foothold to twig. *Still got my orangutan moves,* he crows, rigging a harness. The loggers move in; mother sends her distress call across the web.

KA Rees

BOND DRONE

When I grow up I don't want to be a Bond girl, no. I want to be Bond's drone. Then I will execute the shots: gimbal yaw, pitch, & roll, or dolly zoomed using the adjustment dial to circle the subject sliding those joy sticks around—creating an invisible lasso to pull the subject in tight; measuring the inside seam of his satin slim-fit tuxedo leg: slowly panning up, panning down. *The loving energy of Intelligent Life Batteries™ used to best effect with Hero Gear™.* Don't forget the hard case full of spares for that panoramic over-the-ocean shot, where the orcas float to raid domesticated antibiotic-fed salmon; their sonar pierced by the shrieking alarms fishermen have set to the sides of their net-pens to disrupt the orcas' hunting instincts & give them headaches for weeks. Killers in their Bond tuxedos, black & white matriarchs using familiar research boats to hide behind & sneak up on their prey. Bond grandmas & bond mamas with their bond babies swimming the wide waters; teaching where to look for salmon, safe places to rest & give birth & the best passages to chase the light across oceans.

Jude Bridge

KILLER NIGHT

A cloud of damp grey misogyny rose from the dark streets and floated into my big fuck off car's windows as I saw the dame standing on the side of the road. She had a scarf over her hair and a body so hot that if you pissed on her, she'd still be steaming in the morning. Despite the fact that I had bourbon to drink and a problem with the camera guy, who kept filming the less pleasing side of my face, I pulled over.

'Where you going?' she asked.

'Depends who's asking.'

'I got a problem.'

Sure she did, and she told me that problem was a husband who didn't like the way she vacuumed the house. Left stripes in the living room carpet, didn't vacuum under the rug in the study, forgot to empty the bag.

'Why don't you leave him?' I asked.

She turned away from me, the camera guy following the prettiest side of her face, damn him to hell.

'It's complicated,' she said.

'The situation?'

'No, the vacuum cleaner.'

I drove off into the night, leaving the camera guy, the dame and this voice-over narration limp and lifeless under my big fuck-off tyres.

Ali Jane Smith

HARD CASES

True Detective Phantom Detective Dime Detective Spicy Detective Detective Weekly Suspect Detective Fiction Detective Fiction Weekly Detective Story Detective Story Magazine Private Detective FBI Detective Amazing Detective Special Detective Popular Detective Thrilling Detective True Detective Thrilling Mystery Crack Detective Clues Shocking Detective Stories Exciting Mysteries Detective Spicy Detective Master Detective Detective Cases Detective Book The Gangster Real Detective Ten Detective Aces The Smell of Murder G Men Terror Crime Busters Complete Detective Novel Magazine Smashing Detective Black Mask All Detective Women Crime The Corpse That Walked Human Detective Masked Detective Triple Detective Ellery Queen's Mystery Magazine Detective Short Stories National Detective Speed Mystery Dynamic Detective Flynn's Weekly Space Detective Fast Action Detective and Mystery New Detective Startling Detective Front Page Detective Pay-Off In Blood Two Complete Detective Books Top Notch Detective Headquarters Detective Strange Detective T As In Trapped Detective Tales Daring Detective Simon Lash Private Detective Crime and Violence The Unconscious Witness.

Stuart Barnes

LITTLE GILT

After Charles Marelles & Edgar Allan Poe

Once upon a bleary midnight, a fearless young man with a buzz cut bewitchingly gold as his grandfather's entered The Wood, where flirty older men were frisking about to soulful house. Raoul gently shouldered past these bears and cubs then parted purple curtains, revealing a cheery cocktail lounge. 'Shot of Goldschläger, please.' The lone wolf stood aside and tilted his head. 'Boy oh boy, you're a ray of sunshine.' Raoul noted the hairy arms, the big tongue, the oiled mutton chops; remembered the rough voice, the searing *'Little Lamb'*, the vase of wilted Easter daisies. His foot kept time with the snare drum. 'Two more, please. No, no—one for me, one for my friend with the great white teeth.' Not a single bit of alcohol was spilt. 'Water!' bleated the wolf, scouring the bar as if he'd gulped yellow coals. *Piece of cake*, Raoul thought, emerging from the belly of the club. A neon sign—Pallas, a built centaur—speared its glow around him. *'Police, Fire or Ambulance?'* Raoul called his father next. 'Nevermore,' he said to the pretty stars, disposing of body parts and nursery rhyme, shards of flowers, glass and guilt. The black Sonata drew nearer. 'Nevermore.'

Brenda Proudfoot

SHARED PATHWAY

In the lake, beside the path, a white egret stalks the shallows.

'Mummmyyyy!'

'Sebastian, come here ... he won't hurt her, you know. He's so good with children.'

'It's OK, darling – the doggy's gone now. Do you want to ride your bike?'

'Jeez, did you see how fast that guy was going? Had to be doing 30k at least.'

'Bloody bikewit! Didn't even ring his bell!'

'Youse pair are doing all right. You're going at a fair speed.'

'Caught anything?'

'Nah, that's why it's called fishing not catching.'

Over there ... on that rock. A pied cormorant with wings outspread. A preacher blessing his flock.

Soles scuff on the pavement as a weary jogger goes by.

'I haven't told him how I feel. He says ...'

'Passing on the right.'

'It's osteoarthritis, I think. He cries when he jumps on the bed ...'

'Hey — you going to pick that up?'

The rumble of a skateboard. A teenager careers past, eyes glued to his phone.

See how the pelican lands with outstretched wings. His feet, like lifted skis, barely make a ripple.

Josephine Taylor

SEE WHAT YOU MADE ZEUS DO (PART 1)

Zeus snapped the reins of the chariot and the horses sped towards Olympus. Zeus felt restored to himself after the unpleasantness with Hera, satisfied with the afternoon's ravishing. He chuckled. Transforming himself into a white bull and coaxing Europa onto his back had been a clever trick. Sure, she'd screamed when she realised she was being abducted, cried later and said he'd hurt her. But he knew she'd get over it. They always did. Besides, didn't he deserve a little fun? Ruler of the heavens was a tough gig, what with pronouncing oracles, ordering the heavenly bodies, quashing rebellions... He imagined how it must have gone, the recent conspiracy against him, Hera plotting with the others. Remembered again waking, bound by rawhide thongs – the helplessness. Heard again the Olympians jeering *full of yourself* and *sulk when you don't get your way*. Well he'd taught them all a lesson, hadn't he? Hurled thunderbolts; paid out on his wife. Just remembering how she'd begged as he tied an anvil at each ankle and hung her from the sky returned the smile to his lips. Next, a banquet of nectar and ambrosia. He'd shown her who was boss, now he'd keep her sweet.

Maddie Godfrey

TINY HOUSE FOR SALE: PERFECT FIT FOR YOU AND YOUR MUSE

welcome, come in. the important thing about tiny houses is you must remember to close unnecessary doors. see here – how the kitchen wall becomes a concealed cupboard. there's so much storage beneath the sustainably sourced ivory sink! but if you leave that bathroom door ajar, the hallway becomes an obstacle course of impossibilities. the owner? an architect, skilled at squeezing stories into small spaces. through that archway you'll find the compostable couch. duck! – fuck. sorry, the previous muse was significantly shorter than you. slumped shoulders, perhaps. her head bowed like permanent prayer. more about the architect? a minimalist. likes his coffee black and his women quie– sorry! nothing important, just mumbling to myself. that's right! this *is* that famous house from that famous video! see how the bed folds down like a sarcophagus? how the stairs are shaped like sharpened tongues? and the garden is located on the roof, where you can't water it without risking yourself. all these tiny details, they really paint a persona onto the pine ceilings. isn't it a bargain? we – they – just need a quick sale. you must remember to close unnecessary doors. otherwise you can't esca – I mean, stand up straight.

Susan McCreery

PLAY IT FOR ME

The coffee tasted bitter. But wasn't she in Casablanca drinking gin with Victor? Her head was spinning. She couldn't remember her name. Ilsa or Alicia? They sounded so similar. *You must remember this*. That corny old tune again. Maybe she *was* hungover. *That's not your coffee*, they were saying. *That's Alicia's*. And then it came to her. She was an American agent in Rio. Devlin, her contact, had said he loved her. But he'd passed her over to Alexander, and when Alex asked for her hand, Dev never once said *you don't have to do this*. Instead, he said *a man doesn't tell a woman what to do*. What a load of hooey. They must be poisoning her. She couldn't see through the fog, or was it her hair flying across her eyes? But this was a clammy, swirling fog, the type you get at airports at night. The type you get when you don't know who you are anymore, or which man you're supposed to belong to. Rick was passing her over to Victor. Rick had turned his back, was leaving with Louis. Was it her cue to cry again?

Hilary Hewitt

YOUR LOVED ONE™

We offer whole-of-life pet care for your peace of mind. Our dedicated team of animal-lovers will collect your special companion or take advantage of our convenient downtown drop-off point. Endangered species not accepted. Limit of two larger animals – horse, cow, llama, donkey, etc. 5-star accommodation. Season-appropriate bedding. Enrichment toys, including home-crafted cat dancers, organically sourced chews, themed music, aromatherapy. Our unique Green Cuisine includes vegan, gluten-free and paleo (see *Menu Options*). Our smiling receptionist Aimee-Lee (favourite animal, the goose) is waiting to take your call. No credit or refunds. Personalised Zoom Counselling available 24/7, helping you adjust in advance to your loss (Indian language groups a speciality). We also offer estate management including garden maintenance, in-house pet care and property sale or rent. Our accredited lawyer (favourite animal, the mongoose) is on hand to guide you through the intricacies of leaving your world in safe hands. And when their time comes, our joyful embalmer (favourite animal, the snake) will fix a permanent wag on your little friend's tail before laying them to rest in our whispering glades, forever thinking of you.

Jane O'Sullivan

PORTALS

The cat had discovered a portal to another world, tucked behind the neighbour's shed. He kept bringing home strange things: jellyfish, gobbets, possibly an arm. She wrapped the bits in paper and put them in the bin. Some wars start as easily as that, with a sigh.

Erin Gough

SUPERPOWER REVEAL

The day they assigned our superpowers we were sitting on the deck. Geoff had made margaritas and Pavani and I had ordered pizza to celebrate Geoff's new job at the caryard. That's when the fortune cookies strapped to cocktail umbrellas floated down above our heads.

Geoff's arrived first. He dropped the umbrella into his drink, cracked the cookie and read the message: *Can communicate with reptiles*. 'Yes!' he cried.

Pavani went next. She ate her cookie and pulled the slip of paper from her mouth: *Can see through double brick*. She punched the air, victorious.

Now we had proper reason to celebrate. I tucked my cookie into my bra for later and we headed to the pub for another round of margaritas.

It was dark by the time we got home, so it took us a moment to work out what had happened to the house. We walked closer and saw the breach in the earth, the soil tumbling into the sinkhole. There was the roof, a hundred feet below us. 'What's your super-power, Anna?' Pavani asked hopefully. Maybe I could fix this.

I opened my cookie, holding my breath.

Can translate Latin into fifteen modern languages, I read aloud.

Moya Costello

SPLITTING HAIRS

Northern Rivers had violent accidents and serious crimes.

A head was decapitated. In an interview with Detective David Calla awash with world-weariness, the hairdresser perp said that she'd cut the hair off one too many dickheads. So she cut off a head.

Calla found himself sympathetic: the crime made sense. So much so, he couldn't bring himself to read her the act, take a statement, have her sign it.

He left the room to his 'good cop' ensemble performer.

Besides, he had a good hairdresser.

Danielle Baldock

451 - LIFE, BURNING

Flames eat words faster than she can read them. If she pauses to blow on her icy fingers, whole sentences disappear.

She snatches back a black-frilled page, yelps.

His eyes flicker. What happened?

Burnt my fingers...

He smiles, kisses her hand. That's what you get for reading too slow!

She's used all their stock of firebricks, newspapers pulped and compressed into lumpy rectangles that burn with a clear blue light.

Now she starts on her precious collection of books, her least favourite first.

She holds off as long as she can, but as ice hieroglyphs the windows, and his breath grows ragged, she forces herself at last to her favourites.

She reads them aloud, murmuring as she feeds them to the hungry flames.

Images of their old life burst into being in the bare room, before they're consumed. Dreams of marshmallows and baked potatoes glow in the hissing flames.

He grows stiller, quieter, as she picks up another book.
Strokes its cover, puts it to her nose to smell the familiar papery smell. Bites her lip as she rips the first page.
She chokes then, takes a deep, deep breath, and feeds the brave precious words into the flames.

Cheryl Rogers

VERMIN

'*Ratsak* or *Rat Blitz*?' monotones the Goth slumped over the cash register. '*Blitz* contains Warfarin...thins their blood.'

Tilly knows all about Warfarin. On account of her Nan's arteries.

'One of each,' her customer Nell Graves beams.

The till chick cranks open one kohl-rimmed eyelid. Glances at Nell. Anorak. Wellies. *Trolley load of budget chook feed. Grinning like a fucking axe murderer.*

'Pellets or wax blocks?'

'Pellets,' Nell deadpans. 'George might suspect something if I try to feed him lumps of wax.'

George Graves popped his clogs years back. His temporary resurrection causes the faintest flicker on the pale moon face.

'I'll get Steve to load your car.'

Nell hears the girl's flip flops smacking past pallets of kitty litter and extortionately priced pine shavings.

Soon Steve appears, face flushed, jumpy. Nell's heard business is down. There's talk of staff cuts.

'Reckon her old man's safe?' Tilly asks Steve later, handing him his tea.

'Safe as any man, six feet down,' he responds, sharpish.

The girl's a liability. He'll tell her, as soon as he can shake this headache, find the right words.

Tilly pats her Nan's blister pack in her pocket and watches, waiting for the axe to fall.

Marjorie Lewis Jones

FEVER TALE

While the sink piles and the taps dry and the lamps hiss and the mirror flattens and the walls dampen and the carpet ripples and the air passes through her, the sound is a conch or a fridge or some pressurised underwater breathing, the sleeves hang, the pants dribble from her hips, the shoes slap, the fingers crack, she believes she can see bone, she believes the sea is a ship, the ship is her bed, her bed is a rock, her rock is a shore, her shore is some alien isle she's washed up on, panting and shuddering at the gales, blacked out by the sky that rides above her, raked by tides, scored by shells, wrecked on the sand with her belly heaving, and the nights hurling up bilge-water, spitting grit, she is passed over by the birds at great distances, her skeleton and her eyes are whitening in this viscid asylum where the mist drips blister packs, droops soup, screws bruises into her glittering fears, pulverises her citric hip-joints, steeps onion in her spine, and a sweaty pot of Vicks slips, descends into glass, no soft landing, jags slate, as the fever breaks.

Thomas Simpson

THE SWAP

Family SUVs squeak over speedbumps and thread back onto the highway. They had time on the way south to sample chocolate and wine from deceased industry towns now opt for fast food and faster speed limits of the highway home. Some grimace empathetically at my open bonnet, grease covered hands. In this beehive of movement, I see others left static. Two boys quietly resigned to their burgers and chips. Unkempt hair and muddied feet show the wilful fatigue of a weekend out of town. Their father doesn't eat, fiddles with his phone. It beeps and he's up, pats their heads and leaves. The older boy watches him adjust his shorts by the dusty ute. A woman takes up a seat. The younger takes in her greeting, doesn't notice their backpacks at her feet. She pinches a chip from the older who still watches the ute. He takes in the scene bordered in grey plastic of the rear-view mirror, bows his head, slides the ute into gear. The RAC van pulls up. Roadside assistance now inconvenient, I look beyond the mechanic's baldness for a second thought, an embrace, a tear. I see the playground now faded and derelict, the dull brick service centre resurfaced with smooth marble and glass.

Jan Dean

A SPANISH SCENE

Julie's art gallery nestles between the mountains and the sea. Maria shows her paintings there, and the latest convey scenes of Spain.

Charles is a regular visitor and sometimes buyer. Today he drools in front of one of Maria's recent paintings, depicting a potted geranium on a windowsill. The window, framed by shutters, opens onto a narrow street where stark white buildings are decorated with black wrought iron balconies on upper levels. Crimson geraniums hang in pots, dotted around the walls. Diminishing roof lines lead to a Baroque cathedral's bell tower against a sky of brilliant blue. The street is paved with cobblestones. Wearing a frilled skirt, a woman dancing Flamenco, would not be unexpected.

The painting certainly has impact. *I want this,* Charles blurts. *I'm in love with it,* he moans. *Actually, I'm in love with the artist. I can see her: She's a goddess; tall, willowy, voluptuous and exotic. Her long dark hair curls to her waist. Please arrange an introduction.*

His description is so far from Maria's appearance, Julie bites her lip. Being a superior salesperson she remains circumspect.

Tonight, Charles will dream his heart flames so much for Maria, the phone in his shirt-pocket melts.

Dorothy Simmons

WRITING FOR GODOT

It is a truth universally acknowledged that the path of true love, true crime and true adventure never did run smooth. Romcom and Doreen must defy the slings and arrows of outrageously feuding families to consummate their passion. Sherlock Holmes and Bond (James Bond) must defeat the villainy of the Moriartys and Goldfingers of this world to earn their after dinner port or martini (shaken, not stirred). Tintin and Luke Skywalker must risk life and limb, not to mention the faithful Snowy and R2D2, in order to save the universe. Again.

It keeps them busy. It keeps their authors even busier, writing and rewriting in total faith that one day their Publisher will come and see for the first time what a gem he is denying all the lonely readers; the path to publication has rarely been pottered along smoothly.

When they are not writing and rewriting, the authors pass their time talking to Vladimir and Estragon (Didi and Gogo). They talk about where they have been and what they did yesterday and what they are doing now. They are waiting for Godot. He sent a message that he couldn't come today, but he'd come tomorrow. Without fail. Again.

Anne Booty

WHEN HANNI MET (BUFFALO) BILLY

He waited patiently. A butterfly, singular and beatific, lay thumping in his belly. He sighed. Hannibal was late. Texted to say he was picking up a Chianti. Bill had replied with a thumbs up despite knowing he wouldn't find one at this hour.

Although they'd spent time together online, this would be their first meeting.

In the flesh.

The table was laid with a single layer of translucent skin so as to not hide the poetry of knife marks underneath. Too many and it's like peering through mud! When his date arrived, empty handed, Bill was struck by his strange mask until he remembered there was a Pandemic Out There. How kind of him to be so respectful, he thought. They were shy with each other at first, until Hannibal was given a tour and allowed to peer into the pit. The girl shuddered as she looked up at them, pleading, something in her hands perhaps meat, perhaps her own broken fingernails. I'll have what she's having, Hannibal joked. The words were lost, smothered by mask. Bill smiled awkwardly and led him to the dinner table; his date walking close behind, licking his chops.

Shady Cosgrove

SELF-RESTRAINT

I watch from the window. The zombies are drilling and hammering. It looks like a ramp. Maybe a skate park. Yes, they've built a skate park in the driveway next door. Scooters, boards – there must be eight, nine, ten zombies slicing along the concrete. They spill onto the road but no one cares, no one has parked here in months.

The zombies go shopping. They come home with cases of beer and extra packs of toilet paper, but they are laughing, high-fiving each other.

Tonight, the zombies bring couches and arm chairs out to the street, line them up in tight rows. A screen has been erected at the end of the block so my cul de sac is now an outdoor cinema. Someone has ordered pizza. The zombies drink beer and make toasts, shouting over each other as the opening credits begin. I love this movie, but someone coughs, splutters.

It's well past midnight now and they're running up and down the road, shrieking and whooping. I peek through the curtains. They are falling on the verge in front of my house, giggling and making out.

Michael Brown

COOKIES

The mortar and pestle had been a gift from her vegan friend, an encouragement of sorts, to stop buying herbs and spices in conveniently capped containers that stand upright like soldiers in a rack. The mortar and pestle have sat ornamentally, on her kitchen shelf, until now.

She takes the pestle in her hand, spares a thought to exotic fiction, then with her other hand drops in the first character.

Count Dracula ... is smashed with the heavy stone

In she tosses Spock ... then Chewbacca

Smashed and ground

Rapunzel ... Snow White

Both smashed

Pip ... Boo Radley. Smashed

Holden Caulfield ... 007 ... Ishmael

All of them smashed

When the mortis is full she picks up the mash and rolls it in her hands like a ball of dough. It's fattened by falsehoods that ring true, sweetened by drama and bonded by poetry.

She tears it into walnut sized pieces, sets them evenly over the baking tray and pops it all into the oven.

She will sneak these cookies onto plates at dull parties or share with special friends, but mostly she will nibble on them alone in her quiet spot with a pot of tea.

Beth Spencer

BENEFITS

We cut our eye teeth on each other's hearts.

That letter of yours, late at night — what was that? Best forgotten. So now I love the smooth wall of your skin. Pushing me away, inviting me in. Well-protected, your ribs, a cage. You make sex a game, a twist. Word-play: foreplay.

Always the rules (so safe). Such a trick to find the soft centre in that fist of hard words.

My need for adventure. Your need for conquest.

(And that strangely intimate linking of hands. And those words we must never speak, written, late at night.)

Too long caught in a gauze too thick to untangle. Each wound deep and red again.

Your hand over my mouth.

Your letter, hidden, in plain sight.

Jenni Nixon

TIMES THEY CHANGE

Twas a dark and windy night when woken by sounds unusual. Driven out to investigate from the safety of bed. A crash and boom, the back gate swung open. Rustling, clucking shrieks from the hen house soon follow. A shadow falls from out the dark gives me this night a fright. Takes a leap to bring him down right. Thin fella, no meat on these bones alright.

Deals for mining mates and the military done as a virus of poverty spread thru the land soon stun. Infamy, unemployed on the move seeks jobs where they're none.

'Just wanted a few eggs to feed my family. Chook came running at me, pecks at my throat. Had a knife, sliced to save my life.'

'I've lost my head. Where are we going? Cannot see what's ahead. Neck in a bucket, like a Hills Hoist round in circles my feet run. Play me no sad songs. King Rooster, old cock-boiler is dead. No respect, gone.'

Told Rowdy don't you show your face in this town again. Gave him the carcass, a few eggs to take home. Apology to Bob Dylan but this twas Murder Most Fowl.

Jane Hall

AUNTS VS ZOMBIES

"Good morning students.

Today we are going to learn about the British-inspired AABC, or the 'Aunty-Australian Broadcasting Corporation', its audience and the broader Australian demographic.

Its audience, dubbed by sociologists as the 'Teeveetubbies', love to watch programmes like the deeply spiritual 'Compost', the new and fresh 'Spick and Span', and the gardening lifestyle show 'Get a Life Australia'. They also hang out for their favourite song 'We are None, We are Any'. A diverse group, they are represented on screen by characters like Winky-Winky with his handbag; Tipsy who is a bit radical; dotty but kind Laa-Laa Land, and Poface, the red commy who seems to be a quiet, inoffensive Teeveetubbie.

If only the world was full of such lovely people. But because of its charter, the AABC has to portray what sociologists call the 'Zombies'. They rarely watch TV at all, preferring to trawl the Dark Web and listen to Death Metal. They are about as diverse as a room full of identical twins, and are represented on the AABC by characters like Pauline Tantrum, Barnaby Joyless, Andrew Dolt and the Neo-Nasty Patriotic Defence League for United Nationalist Freedom Zombies.

Any questions?"

Sam Andrews

A MARVELLOUS NIGHT

Dense fog covers the barren moor. Moonbeams dance, strands of silver swirling in the vapour. Rocky ground lies wet underfoot; treacherous. Any wrong step delivers a plunge into the circling bog that sucks and swallows hungrily. Beware! A peat-filled grave.

Howling. Howling in the dark. Then, the thud, thudding of a heart. Wild eyes roll, frosted ears strain. Was the inhuman baying in front or behind? Best keep running or better to hide? Are those boulders... a cave? Howling in the dark.

Boots heavy with mud, rise and fall. The cave mouth opens, swallowing the prey; his crimes committed regularly: travelling fools who wander villages after dusk should be robbed, should be beaten. This one had looked soft, tasty in the warmth of the tavern's fire. Knowing faces were averted as he followed the boy outside. Leering, creeping, closer. Greedy, grasping fingers outstretched. Then, the moon, and *Transformation*. Horror of horrors; a milk-fed boy becomes the creature of nightmares!

Now, cowering in the dark. A besieged swine in its house of stone, but not alone. Yellow eyes open, burning with anticipation. Moist, urgent breath envelops a shivering nape. Realisation dawns; too late to flee. Blood fountains over the beast's maw.

Hannah Cockroft

DUCK

The husbands of the village take turns to spit at me as I'm carried to the end of the pier. I make a show of trying to squirm free from the ropes that bind me to the ducking stool, but these men spend 8 months of the year at sea, and are able to tie knots with the same precision and dexterity with which they stroke themselves to ecstasy. I am dangled over the edge of the water, black and beckoning. The men announce the accusations against me, deciding that my nature must be tested.

Depending on the result, I will be either left to the sea or set alight. *Their* fate is already set. The stool is lowered, and I am sure to smile at the crowd in gratitude. They are sending me home.

As the saltwater surrounds me, my body undulates from its guise, the ocean washing away this mortal flesh. I am finally ready to complete the task that their wives summoned me for.

Although I will certainly feast heartily, some of the younger ones will look so pretty as they float, anchored to my sandy bed, preserved forever in the brine.

Seetha Nambiar Dodd

THE SISTERHOOD OPENS A WINDOW OF OPPORTUNITY

From: the_sisters@grimm.org
To: snow_white@thesevendwarves.com
Subject: Version 2.0

Snow, I need to reach out and touch base ASAP. Your predicament is a significant pain point for the Sisterhood, yet you are strangely jovial, evidenced by your singing while sweeping that mini prison you call home. (Incidentally, sweeping is now obsolete. A best-of-breed vacuum cleaner would be a game changer for hoovering the crumbs of untidy dictators.)

Nevertheless, you need a paradigm shift, Snow. Yes, you've been giving it 110% but isn't it time to start thinking outside the box? Raise the bar! Do you want to spend your days at the beck and call of seven bosses just to live rent-free? *It is what it is* does not align with our mission statement. Let's empower you! Let's get the ball rolling before the goalposts are moved and you are locked in.

Time to act! This train is pulling out of the station (at 10 tomorrow morning). I'll get all your ducks in a row and you can say goodbye to each one before we jump ship and get onboard.

Forget the Prince, Snow. At the end of the day, he's a non-starter. Let me reconceptualise your story.

Change is coming.

Nick Couldwell

OILSKIN

His oilskin jacket hangs inside the cupboard beside the old water heater. I had seen him wear it, seen him use it for things one shouldn't talk about. He loved it with a fondness that saddened me. He loved it like a brother, as if they had shared secrets and unbearable truths, and he let it weigh down across his shoulders like a friendly arm after a win at the races. He wished to be laid to rest adorned in this sheath, his lifeless body mummified and protected by its history. It had weathered its share of animal shit and tractor grease, upset port, blood. It was unmistakably durable. With enough force, a taut sleeve could easily collapse a grown man's windpipe. Render a trachea unusable.

There's a specially designed pocket on the inside breast to keep spare brass buttons and dislodged teeth. If you can hold a person rigid and still for long enough, the tiny stitched rectangle will map an inch-perfect position of the heart.

It's stated somewhere, on the jacket itself or otherwise, that it's wind resistant, water resistant, breathable. At his grave, I bless myself and touch the oilskin like it's my very own.

Adria Castellucci

SEA FOAM, REDUX

'I'm ready.'

The Sea Witch opened her eyes and stared at the Mermaid, saying nothing.

'I mean it this time.'

The Sea Witch sighed. 'How many times have you come to me in the middle of the night, then swum straight back to your father's kingdom? You have no idea what you want.'

The Mermaid flushed; her silver scales trembled with defiance. 'I'm not leaving.'

The Sea Witch swam closer, the ripples of her wake lapping against the Mermaid's skin. 'You realise you can never return? They won't accept you back.'

The Mermaid swallowed, nodded. The Sea Witch retreated to the depths of her cave; returned with a string of fat, lustrous pearls.

'What's this?' the Mermaid asked.

'Something I've been keeping for you.'

The Mermaid bit her lip, pulled back the floating curtain of her hair. The Sea Witch's fingers brushed against her neck. The necklace's clasp clicked into place.

'What do you think? The Sea Witch wrapped her tentacles around the Mermaid. 'Do you like them?'

The Mermaid tried to speak, but no sound came out. Then her lips met the Sea Witch's, and she found her voice.

'My love.'

They drifted down to the ocean floor.

Sky Carrall

DOWN THE CREEK

My friend Jam once told me it can't be sunny every day.

It was just something she said while we were down the creek, waiting for the bell. Clarks discarded on the bank, we laid top to tail on a rock midstream, our legs dangling off the edges.

'Hey Poppy?'

I turned my head, absorbing the rock's warmth into my cheek. She faced the sky with closed eyes. I stared into her ear canal, wondering if it really was possible to dig your finger in close enough to touch your brain.

'What do you want to be when you grow up?' she asked.

'Don't know.'

'What about when you were little?'

I didn't want to say. The creek dribbled below, parting at our small island, rejoining at the other side. 'I used to want to be an astronaut,' I confessed.

'That's hard. Maybe a weatherwoman?'

'That's not the same.'

She smiled, eyes still shut. I closed mine too and saw the backs of my eyelids glow pink as the sunlight beamed over. 'Maybe I'll just lie on rocks under the sun for a living,' I said.

'Just like this?'

I nodded.

'It can't be sunny every day.'

Suzanne Frankham

WASTE NOT WANT NOT

Ingredients
A pinch of covid-19 boredom
A touch of second lockdown madness
Lashings of housewifely guilt
Homegrown windfall oranges
Sugar to taste
A setting agent

Method
• Salvage any early windfall oranges lying around the tree. Discard if skin broken or infested with insects.
• Leave in the pantry where fermentation and softening continue.
• When guilt sets in, and grandmother's words, waste not, want not, echo in the brain, roll on bench to promote the release of juices (a kneading motion).
• Juice oranges. (Preferably coerce some male in house to assist).
• Discard pips.
• Boil until approximately half the volume.
• Taste.

• Since windfall oranges are sour, add sugar to sweeten.

• Follow instructions on packet of gelatine (or other setting agent), to determine amount to use. If past use-by date, increase by half.

• Dissolve in boiling orange juice.

• Pour into jelly mould and set.

• Unmould onto plate, serve with any decorations available, such as tinsel and sparklers.

Rating: ★☆☆☆☆

Comments: Disgusting. Windfall oranges are bitter. Sugar cannot disguise this fact. Consider adding vodka and turning into jelly shots, where taste is a secondary consideration, and the chance of enjoyment greatly enhanced.

Art OBrien

MY LORD

Federica De Gules had, after much effort, become, a squire to the brave Lord Green, scourge to those evil trolls on the other side of the valley. What did the Trolls know of working, with their cushy jobs and cultural elitism; truly the "city" of Leftish Libertaria was hellish place devoted to the demise of the hardy settlement of Conersitia Liberaterian. The worse thing though was their Dark Lord Helleron, who constantly lied about the corruption of Lord Green.

Glendrex, was just finishing her breakfast and reading the news. Those Trolls and their Dark Lord on the other side of the Valley in Conersitia Liberaterian made her angry. Lord Green was corrupt, and a liar who oppressed the whole valley; but the inhabitants of Consitia Liberaterian refused to admit it.

War had raged for centuries.

Admiral Jefferson was a proudly serving member of the Galactic Collective; as he sat in his cabin aboard his star frigate, he couldn't help but chuckle, didn't the valley dwellers, humans all, know there were real threats like the Galaxy Peacekeepers. Aboard his flagship Admiral Peterson of the Galaxy Peacekeepers was thinking the same thing about the Galactic collective.

Sandra Renew

SUITS

When I was living in a world of the Beatles and a rebellious, wayward Princess, it was a time of romance and hope. Strangely remembered as the 'best time of your life' by suspect uncles and stiffly mannered aunts with life lessons to impart.

Now, in insomniac dreams, I know the Prince danced in strange vibrations — the most desirable thing in the vision being an Italian suit, softly draped fabric, dark over a crisp white cotton shirt and insouciant tie. No words in that age for what was strange or queer, desire for the image. Leave the body out of the picture, or replace it with ambiguity in the suit, or to be honest, both of us in suits and crisp collared shirts. Swoon material! Now we have the words, banal descriptions for same-sex androgyny, two of us on the wedding cake, still in our Cuban-heeled boots and the Italian suits.

Ann Vickery

AN EYRE OF ROMANCE

Brontë Bell born, barter forlorn. Respect one's betters but be no bird. Boisterous with bother, the burdens of teacher and sitter. Bertha's mad flitter, to believe or bewilder. Beaten by banter, gossip burnt her. Border or box, hive off the tox. Barnstoming the blue to broker anew. Brat of my heart, bend it full blast. Be my boo, I burnish for two.

Rosanna Licari

BAD WEATHER

Dad'd go bushwalking alone. Mum'd say *Everyone should be careful in bad weather.* That's for sure. It was a grey, wet day when he vanished. The police scoured the tracks and gullies. Nothing.

It's easier to dig in the garden when it's wet. *You're a good girl* Mum'd say when I helped her after Dad disappeared. At least his beatings stopped. I wanted to burn all his things, but Mum said we needed to show respect for the dead. *Every family has secrets.* She didn't want to lose face.

Years later, just after a big storm, I was down in a spot where she never let me dig. My spade hit something hard. I uncovered old bones. I'd done high school science. I got the picture. I turned and Mum was staring at me, leaning on her walking stick. None of us said a word.

At the kitchen table, I never asked how she got Dad to the bottom of the yard and into the garden bed. You know, the details. She just kept stirring the tea in her cup. She could barely speak. By that time, the cancer had got to her throat and we were used to silence.

Ruth Horsfall

HORNY FOR THE VIRUS

If this virus were a physical assailant, an unexpected and invis-
ible mugger – which I can tell you from personal experience, it
is. I was having to come to terms with the fact that Boris was
horny for the idea of physically fighting a viral disease. Self-
deprecation sits uncomfortably on him, you can tell it makes him
feel constricted, a little breathless. ...shining the light of science
on this invisible killer and we will pick it up when it strikes. It is
very hard to give a speech with a rock hard erection given to
you by yourself by that very speech ... *then this is the moment*
when we have begun together to wrestle it to the floor... the
moment when we can press home our advantage. The virus is
the new boy in the boarding house and Boris has noticed his
soft hands, and dimpled smile. Sometimes the virus talks and
Boris is compelled to reach out and touch him. Boris is waiting
for the right moment to fling the virus to the ground, and if he is
able to see what his hair smells like at the same time, so be it.

Sam Elkin

MEAT TOWER 9

I arrived at work to an all-staff email telling us that we had to move offices. It was the second time this year. I hadn't noticed any water leaks or cracks, but the scaffolding out the front was starting to feel permanent.

As my colleagues and I stood in the elevator with our personal effects in boxes, I realised that the office movers had missed an umbrella I'd left at my desk. I went to fetch it.

When I arrived, the office had already been gutted, and a strange smell hung in the air. I pushed past a "do not enter" sign, and saw the exterior wall being carved off by a huge serrated crane. It plopped fleshily to the ground below. I backed out, mouth agape, and manically headed for the ground floor. As I descended, I opened my phone and read conspiracy theories about secret plans to start growing office towers from DNA-altered bovine stem cells to address dwindling global supplies of steel and arable farming land. I escaped outside, and saw that the building was made entirely of meat; like a super-sized doner kebab rotisserie in the sky, grown to cut building costs and feed us all.

Deborah Van Heekeren

IF ON AN ANXIOUS WEDNESDAY A DREAMER

Teeth crunching, loosening. Lost in the house I had always known. Down a corridor another door, another room. I close my eyes. Pulse racing. Hear his voice – measured, reassuring, easing me gently down. I know it will be over quickly, but there were bad experiences in the past. I brace myself. Let the needle do its work. Creeping numbness so terrifyingly strange. Instant panic. Heart racing. Can't breathe. Want to flee.

"Let's take out that filling and see what's underneath."

The pictures are ugly.

"We have to take up the floor. It's in really bad shape. Very uneven. Sunken in some places. You can't install cupboards. It would be a waste of money. That old timber is rotting. Termites. Dampness. You'd better come and have a look!"

The pictures are ugly.

Mouth stuffed to overflowing. Fingers. Rubber. Suction. Oh god no! That spongy thing I just chewed on was my tongue.

"It will heal quickly."

A *difficult* filling. A dark hole. Damp stinking earth. Hadn't seen the light of day for more than a hundred years. Termite tunnels, a petrified rat, structural collapse.

Time is a healer. Time is a monster.

Mark O'Flynn

FEARLESS

Leaping from the galloping pony onto a runaway train... Hanging from a butcher's hook by the wrists... Walking the tightrope suspended between skyscrapers... Lynch mob on the doorstep... Hairpin bends around the winding mountain pass, roads greasy, brake cables severed... Boiling oil cascading from the ramparts... Laser beam sizzling up the table between your legs... Hostile robots taking over the city... Here, *mein herr,* your choice of cyanide pill... The knock knock of grave dirt on the polished coffin lid, muffled sound of scratching from within... Blackbeard swishing his cutlass makes you walk the plank... Five fathoms down, oxygen tank on empty... Can anyone fly this plane?... Geronimo! Oh no, a hole in the parachute... Firing squad at the ready, aim... Swimming the crocodile infested river, ivory too heavy for the canoe... Lookout, cannibals!... Simmering with carrots in the cooking pot... Thrown into the arena, hungry lions pacing their cage... Beware of the Dobermann... Doomsday clock ticking and only you to decipher the secret code with the answer to everything... Abandoned without water in the desert, champagne all that's left... More bad cholesterol... You and I self-isolating. Thirteen more nights to survive.

Tess Pearson

BLACK ICE

She rose before morning, dressed in low lamplight, and stuffed the duffle bag full. She unbolted the back door and pulled on her boots, still caked with mud from yesterday's reconnaissance. The orange glow of her cigarette intensified with each drag. She stood against the wall, tilting her head back, caressing the scar running ear to mouth. A lone bird cried out. It was time. Today was the sweet day. Her grin pulled taut, teeth peeling into the cold night like ripe fruit being split open. A cackle escaped her. She was ready. Her lips wavered for a moment, threatening grimace. Then, stubbing out the cigarette, she lifted the bag over her shoulder, slung on her hat, and walked round to the street. She unlocked and mounted the fixed wheel, riding into the tender morning. To the unsuspecting eye of commuters, she looked like a cycle courier going about her day. Her intentions lay hidden beneath a semblance of the ordinary, invisible as ice on the road that cold morning. The hard, slick trick of it keeping her balance sharp. The strap of the bag dug into her clavicle, the only telltale sign of the heavy tools inside.

Kate Middleton

REST CURE

Oh, so consumed! A frilled bed skirt. A dimmed room and the soothe of words. A novel— sensational, thrilling. This is malady.

Because *you* are the sickly double. The threat to the underhanded marriage plot, the contract negotiations for upcoming nuptials, inheritance. There's a sneaky accountant, or a malevolent noble, or a pretender to a trustworthy heart. There's theatrical evil, wearing a smoking jacket or a parlour jacket or suede gloves or an elaborate cravat. And you're the woman buried alive, out of public sight. Ache of limbs proves it. Squeal of nerves proves it. Your caretaker is a your keeper. *We're isolating*. And the door is locked to outsiders. Threshold a dangerous place. Asylum within.

In a fit of unrest you'll be wandering the streets, the local park, greet the local dogs, cats, as if a ghost. The paths will disappear, desire lines. Like the twice-daily erasure of the Lindisfarne causeway. As if ailment erases your desires.

Elsewhere a "real" version, the publicly sanctioned self, is conducting transactions. Smiles for a photo. Senses your vigil, somewhere. Your sacrifice.

PS Cottier

TUDES

Nests of paper and cardboard appeared everywhere. Or were carefully constructed by the Tudes, to be more accurate.

The creatures were finger-length wrigglers, who tore up books to make bedding with teeth of a kind unknown in any other worm. They leaked burning liquid from holes at both ends of their bodies, screaming noises that made cockatoos' cries seem sweet. They resembled tube-worms in shape, but the vitriol and screams spoke of attitude. Hence 'tude-worms, then just Tudes.

At the Centre for Errant Entomology we worked out that they only used books with fruit in the title. *Huckleberry Finn. Clockwork Orange. James and the Giant Peach.* Vitamin-rich titles for the toxic Tudes.

They formed cocoons, and we waited. What a relief to see the glorious butterflies! Each was the colour of the fruit in the title of the book it had chosen for its nest. My colleague Andrea was looking at a cherry-coloured wonder that had nested in the remnants of a Chekhov play. It rested on her nose, all flutter and joy.

It spat. Andrea's eyes swelled, and her skin blistered.

Buttertudes have colonised every corner of the country. Such a glorious harvest of fruity pain.

Richard Holt

A CENT AND A HALF

Otis MacIsaac rented an apartment bang in the middle of the 44th Street strip, with a liquor store on street level. During the hot summer of '38 its dingy living room hosted gatherings every Saturday. Crap games and card games. And always talk of stories and editors and dreams of 2-cents-a-word. Selling to *Black Mask*. Breaking into the slicks.

One night, with celebrations in full swing, Otis hauled out his Remington, announcing he'd promised Norton-Taylor at *Detective Fiction* 12,000 words by next morning. Regardless, Otis insisted the party continue. By midnight, chaos all around him, he had a title, a hero, a victim, a twist, and 2,000 words. He called for opinions - an irresistible invitation to a room full of writers. By four he had a complex cast and a plot we all knew had something.

Three months later Hollywood picked up *Cloak of Chaos*. Bogart would play the hero. Otis moved west. Bought himself a Packard. Many who'd been there the night the story was written laid claim to its unforgettable denouement. But stuck, as we were, on a cent and a half a word, we had no time to waste on resentment.

Biographies

SAM ANDREWS has been telling stories his whole life, and now he's writing them down! A Sydneysider who loves dancing with his partner, Sam devotes spare time to shivering timbers, kick-starting hearts, and where appropriate, tickling funnies.

DANIELLE BALDOCK's atmospheric writings capture small and vivid moments of time. She has been published in a trio of Spineless Wonders' anthologies, lives in Sydney and takes lots of photos. Her favourite colour is green.

STUART BARNES's *Glasshouses* (UQP) won the Arts Queensland Thomas Shapcott Prize and was shortlisted/commended for two other awards. 'Off-World Ghazal' was shortlisted for the Montreal International Poetry Prize. He's working on his second collection. @StuartABarnes

Singer, musician, word wrangler. Brisbane-born **ANNE BOOTY** now resides by the sea in England, with a steady supply of vegemite in the cupboard to remind her of home. She likes cats and B-grade movies.

JUDE BRIDGE's monologue "The Joys of Menopause" was chosen, performed and filmed with great style by Baggage Productions in November. Elsewhere, there was a bit of short-listing and she's made friends with a small, elderly pony.

MICHAEL BROWN is a contributing writer for various horticultural journals. He studied creative writing at Long Island University NY. He has self published two books of poetry. Michael lives by the sea in Lennox Head, Australia.

JOANNE BURNS' poetry collections include *apparently*, short-listed for the 2020 NSW Premier's Poetry Award and *brush*, which won the 2016 NSW Premier's Poetry Award. Her poems are studied in high schools and have been produced for radio and theatre.

SKY CARRALL is a Wollongong-based fiction writer. She writes about growing up, friendship and connection, and loves reading coming-of-age and literary fiction. She has previously been published in Spineless Wonders' *Slinkies Shorts 2020* anthology.

ADRIA CASTELLUCCI is a Sydney-based librarian and writing school dropout who is rediscovering a passion for writing after a ten-year hiatus. Her new work explores themes of fairytale, femininity, and queerness.

HANNAH COCKROFT is an emerging Perth-based author and playwright. Her debut play *Talkback* premiered at the Blue Room Theatre in 2020. Her short stories were selected for the 2017 and 2018 *Frankie* Good Stuff Awards.

SHADY COSGROVE is the author of *What the Ground Can't Hold* (Picador) and *She Played Elvis* (Allen and Unwin). Her short works have appeared in *Best Australian Stories, Overland, Antipodes, Southerly*, and Spineless Wonders publications.

MOYA COSTELLO has four books, work in many scholarly and creative journals and anthologies (including from Spineless Wonders), has read at many venues, judged writing competitions and received writing grants. Adjunct lecturer, Southern Cross University.

PS COTTIER writes poetry, short stories, book reviews and essays. Her latest poetry collections are *Monstrous* (Interactive Press) and *Utterly* (Ginninderra Press), both published 2020. She lives in Canberra.

NICK COULDWELL is a writer from Byron Bay. His fiction has appeared in *Best Australian Stories*, *Westerly* and Spineless Wonders. He has three daughters.

JAN DEAN won the 2018 joanne burns Microlit Award, Hunter Region, published in *Shuffle*. Her 2019 entry is published in *Scars*. She won the 2019 Lane Cove Senior Award (for Poetry) published 2020.

SEETHA NAMBIAR DODD is a Malaysian-born, Sydney-based mum of three who loves beautiful sentences. She is fuelled by green tea, white wine and deadlines. Her favourite colour is red and her favourite word is ricochet.

SAM ELKIN is a writer, lawyer and radio maker living in the western suburbs of Naarm. Sam was a 2019 Wheeler Centre Next Chapter fellow, and the creator of the podcasts *Transdemic* and *Transgender Warriors*.

An unexpected traveler, **SUZANNE FRANKHAM** lived in four countries before settling in Melbourne. With a scientific background she spent most of her life constrained by technical jargon but has found the transition to creative writing liberating.

MADDIE GODFREY is a writer, educator and emotional feminist who has performed their poetry at The Sydney Opera House and Glastonbury Festival. Their debut collection *How To Be Held* (Burning Eye Books, 2018) is a manifesto to tenderness. maddiegodfrey.com

ERIN GOUGH is an award-winning writer of short-stories and novels. *The Flywheel* won the Ampersand Prize and *Amelia Westlake* won the Readings Young Adult Book Prize and the NSW Premier's Prize for Young Adult Fiction.

JANE HALL's passion is writing and researching, with achievements including a sociology PhD, a publication and prize for best essay in a national competition.

HILARY HEWITT works as a building designer and heritage consultant in Sydney's inner west. Her microfiction has appeared in Spineless Wonders microlit anthologies and other literary journals and featured in venues around the inner west.

RICHARD HOLT's microfiction collection, *What You Might Find* (Spineless Wonders, 2018) was described by *The Australian*'s Ed Wright as 'a tonic for readers in search of new angles from which to spin the world around in their heads'. Richard creates text-based installations and performances in public spaces.

RUTH HORSFALL is a writer with a day job based in the UK, but grew up a settler on the unceded lands of the Wiradjuri people. She has recently been published in Cordite and *The Blue Nib*.

MARJORIE LEWIS-JONES is an award-winning Sydney writer published by Spineless Wonders, ABC Radio National, Picaro Press, Poetry Australia, *Cordite*, Hunter Writers Centre, *Best Australian Writing 2015*, and other anthologies. She runs the literary blog, abiggerbrighterworld.com

ROSANNA LICARI's work has appeared in various journals and anthologies including *Scars: anthology of microlit* (Spineless Wonders, 2020), and T*he Anthology of Australian Prose Poetry* (MUP, 2020).She is the poetry editor of online journal, *StylusLit*.

SUSAN MCCREERY is the author of three collections (poetry, microfiction, short stories): *Waiting for the Southerly*, *Loopholes* and *This Person Is Not That Person*. She has completed her first novel and is working on her second.

KATE MIDDLETON's *Fire Season* (Giramondo, 2009) was awarded the Western Australian Premier's Award for Poetry in 2009 and *Ephemeral Waters* (Giramondo, 2013) was shortlisted for the NSW Premier's award in 2014. In 2020 she was runner up for the Australian Book Review's Calibre Award.

JENNI NIXON is a writer and performance poet based in Sydney. Her poetry collections include *swimming underground* (Ginninderra Press, 2015) and poetry publication in *Southerly* and *Cordite*.

ART OBRIEN graduated from ANU after studying Political Science and History. He has been a public servant in Canberra since 2008. In his spare time, he attempts to create stories less melodramatic than 2020.

MARK O'FLYNN's latest books are the novel *The Last Days of Ava Langdon* and the short story collection *Dental Tourism* (Puncher & Wattmann, 2020).

JANE O'SULLIVAN is a Sydney-based independent arts writer. Her short fiction has been published in *Mascara*, *Meniscus*, *Island* and *Going Down Swinging* online.

TESS PEARSON is a writer and trainee art therapist living on Gadigal land. Her writing won the NWF/SW joanne burns Microlit Award (2017) and was 2nd runner-up for TLB/RMIT non/fictionLab Prize for Experimental Nonfiction (2019).

BRENDA PROUDFOOT is a Lake Macquarie-based writer of short fiction and poetry, and a former English teacher. Her stories were published in *Shuffle* and *Scars* (Spineless Wonders) and short-listed for the Microflix Writers Award (2020).

KA REES writes poetry and short fiction. Her debut poetry collection, *Come the Bones* is published by Flying Island Press (2021).

SANDRA RENEW's collection, *Acting Like a Girl* (Recent Work Press, 2019) won the 2020 ACT Writing and Publishing Award for Poetry. Her poetry is published widely including in *Griffith Review, Hecate, Axon, Australian Poetry Journal.*

Former journalist **CHERYL ROGERS** spends her writing time plotting crime fiction, co-writing memoir and opposing silly planning. A two time winner at the 2020 Scarlet Stiletto Awards, she is published in Australia, the U.K. and U.S.A.

DOROTHY SIMMONS has always loved language, specifically the power of a few marks on a page to conjure worlds. From Young Adult to historical to short fiction, making myths is how we understand ourselves.

THOMAS SIMPSON is a poet based in Fremantle, WA. He has an MA from Curtin University and is a committee member of WA Poets Inc. His work has appeared in print and online.

ALI JANE SMITH is the author of a chapbook, *Gala* (FIP). Her poems have been published in literary journals, including *Southerly, Overland, Rabbit, Plumwood Mountain* and *Cordite.* Find out more about Ali Jane Smith online at alijanesmith.wordpress.com.

BETH SPENCER's books include *Vagabondage, How to Conceive of a Girl* and *The Party of Life*. Awards include the 2018 Carmel Bird Digital Literary Award for *The Age of Fibs*. Her work has frequently been broadcast on ABC-RN. She lives on Guringai & Darkinjung land. www.bethspencer.com

JOSEPHINE TAYLOR is an Associate Editor at *Westerly* and an Adjunct Senior Lecturer in Writing at Edith Cowan University. Her debut novel, *Eye of a Rook*, was published by Fremantle Press in February 2021.

DEBORAH VAN HEEKEREN was born in Sydney and moved to Maitland in 2013. Since her retirement from a career in anthropology, she has concentrated on a creative practice that brings together poetry and visual art.

ANN VICKERY teaches writing and literature at Deakin University. She is the author of two poetry collections, *The Complete Pocketbook of Swoon* (Vagabond Press, 2014) and *Devious Intimacy* (Hunter Publishers, 2015).

JEN WEBB is Distinguished Professor of Creative Practice at the University of Canberra, and co-editor of the literary journal *Meniscus*. Her most recent poetry collection is *Flight Mode* (with Shé Hawke; Recent Work Press 2020).

Editor

CASSANDRA ATHERTON is an award-winning writer, academic and critic. Her most recent books include *Prose Poetry: An Introduction* (Princeton UP), *Anthology of Australian Prose Poetry* (Melbourne UP), *Fugitive Letters* (Recent Work Press) with Paul Hetherington and Leftovers (Life Before Man).

She has judged many literary awards, including the Victorian Premier's Literary Awards: Prize for Poetry, The Lord Mayor's Prize for Poetry and the *Australian Book Review* Elizabeth Jolley short story competition.

The joanne burns Award

Each year Spineless Wonders auspices an award for the best writing in the forms of prose poem and microfiction in honour of foremost Australian experimental poet, joanne burns. The award is open to people residing in Australia and to Australians living overseas. Finalists chosen by each year's judging panel are offered publication in our annual anthology alongside invited writers.

The inaugural *joanne burns Award* was held in 2011 and was judged by joanne burns who selected Charles D'Anastasi's 'Madame Bovary' as the winning entry and commended Erin Gough's 'William Shatner vows to save the Great Basin Pocket Mouse' and Clare McHugh's 'Briefly'. All three pieces, along with those of other finalists appear in *small wonder*, edited by Linda Godfrey and Julie Chevalier.

The *2012 joanne burns Award* was judged by Carol Jenkins who selected Mark O'Flynn's 'under the maw of luna park' as the winning entry and commended Richard Holt's 'bush burial', Trina Denner's 'playing outside', Stu Hatton's 'down south' and Paul Mitchell's 'The Old Man and the Pool'. The winner and finalists all appear in *Stoned Crows & other Australian Icons*, edited by Julie Chevalier and Linda Godfrey.

The *2013 joanne burns Award* was judged by Shady Cosgrove who selected Mark Smith's '10.42 to Sydenham' as the winning entry and Hilary Hewitt's 'happy' and Mark Robert's 'cities that are not Dublin' as runners-up. All three pieces, along with those of other finalists appear in *Writing to the Edge*, edited by Linda Godfrey and Ali Jane Smith.

In *2014, The joanne burns Award* was judged by Angela Meyer and Richard Holt who selected Susan McCreery's 'Hold Up' as the winning entry and Kirsten Tranter's 'Turing Test Study Guide' and Mark Smith's 'The Meteorologist's Daughter' as runners up. All three pieces, along with those of other finalists are published in *Flashing the Square*, edited by Linda Godfrey and Bronwyn Mehan.

The *2015 joanne burns Award* was judged by Kirsten Tranter who selected Nick Couldwell's 'Dancing' as the winning entry. Runners up were Tim Heffernan for 'Butterflies in Iraq' and Matthew Gabriel for 'jesussaves82'. All three pieces, along with those of other finalists and invited contributors are published in *Out of Place* edited by Kirsten Tranter and Linda Godfrey.

The *2016 joanne burns Microlit Award* was co-sponsored by the Newcastle Writers Festival. The national category, judged by Cassandra Atherton, was won by Tim Heffernan for 'Barunga Conversation' and the Newcastle category, judged by Karen Whitelaw and Joanna Atherfold Finn, was won by Dael Allison for 'Breakwall'. The winning entries and finalists from both catego-ries as well as invited contributors are published in *Landmarks* edited by Cassandra Atherton.

The 2017 joanne burns Microlit Award was co-sponsored by the Newcastle Writers Festival and judged by Cassandra Atherton. The national category was won by Tess Pearson for 'Traces' and the Hunter category was won by Luke Evans for 'You Can't Go Back'. The winning entries and finalists from both categories as well as invited contributors are published in *Time* edited by Cassandra Atherton.

The 2018 joanne burns Microlit Award was co-sponsored by the Newcastle Writers Festival and judged by Cassandra Atherton. The national category was won by Brenda Saunders for 'Birding' and the Hunter category was won by Jan Dean for 'Fish Flops and Flaps'. The winning entries and finalists from both categories as well as invited contributors are published in *Shuffle* edited by Cassandra Atherton.

The 2019 joanne burns Microlit Award was co-sponsored by the Newcastle Writers Festival and judged by Cassandra Atherton. The national category was won by K A Rees for 'No White M & Ms' and the Hunter category was won by Shaynah Andrews for 'The Ocean Has Made Promises'. The winning entries and finalists from both categories as well as invited contributors are published in *Scars* edited by Cassandra Atherton.

The 2020 joanne burns Microlit Award was co-sponsored by the Newcastle Writers Festival and judged by Cassandra Atherton. The national category was won by Jane O'Sulivan for 'Portals' and the Hunter category was won by Deborah Van Heekeren for 'If on an anxious Wednesday a dreamer'.

Winning entries and finalists from both categories as well as invited contributors are published in *Pulped Fiction* edited by Cassandra Atherton.

About joanne burns

joanne burns grew up in Sydney's eastern suburbs. She worked as an English teacher in New South Wales, and for a time in London. She has taught creative writing in tertiary institutions, schools and community organisations. Her first collection of poems, *Snatch*, was published in London in 1972. Since then she has published more than a dozen further books of poetry. Her poems have appeared in numerous Australian literary journals, poetry magazines and have been set for study on the Higher School Certificate syllabus. joanne has been particularly concerned with the blurring of the distinctions between poetry and prose in her work, and has written extensively in prose poem/ microfiction forms. She has also written monologues and short futurist fictions and 'farables' (fables/ parables). Her latest collection *Brush* was published by Giramondo Poets in 2014. In 2016, she was awarded the New South Wales Premiers' Kenneth Slessor Literary Award for Poetry. A new collection of her work 'apparently' will be published by Giramondo Poetry in 2019.

Acknowledgements

Spineless Wonders would like to warmly thank the following authors invited by Professor Cassandra Atherton to contribute to *Pulped Fiction*: joanne burns, Shady Cosgrove, Nick Couldwell, Erin Gough, Tess Pearson, KA Rees, Thomas Simpson, Josephine Taylor, Jen Webb, Richard Holt, Ann Vickery and Ali Jane Smith.

We also wish to express our appreciation to the Newcastle Writers Festival and its Director, Rosemarie Milsom for the ongoing support for The joanne burns Microlit Award.

Find more microlit at
SPINELESS WONDERS
www.shortaustralianstories.com.au

Spineless Wonders publications are available in print, digital and audio format from participating bookshops and online. For further information, go to the Spineless Wonders website:

www.shortaustralianstories.com.au